Percy B. Shelley, Clara M. J. Clairmont

Letters from Percy Bysshe Shelley to Jane Clairmont

Percy B. Shelley, Clara M. J. Clairmont

Letters from Percy Bysshe Shelley to Jane Clairmont

ISBN/EAN: 9783337388119

Printed in Europe, USA, Canada, Australia, Japan

Cover: Foto ©Andreas Hilbeck / pixelio.de

More available books at **www.hansebooks.com**

LETTERS

FROM

PERCY BYSSHE SHELLEY

TO

JANE CLAIRMONT.

1889.

London : Privately Printed.

(*Not for Sale.*)

CONTENTS.

———

CONTENTS.

LETTERS,

LETTERS TO
JANE CLAIRMONT.

LETTER I.

LONDON
Dec. 30, 1816.

DEAREST CLARE

YOUR letter to-day relieved me from a weight of painful anxiety.—Thank you too my kind girl for not expressing much of what you must feel, the loneliness and the low spirits which arise from being entirely left.—Nothing could be more provoking than to find all this unnecessary :—However they will now be satisfied and quiet.—

We cannot come to-morrow, there being no inside place in any of the

coaches or in either of the mails. I
have secured a place for Wednesday—
the day following that on which you
will receive this letter—so that you will
infallibly see us on that evening. I may
say that it was by a most fortunate
chance that I secured the places that
I did.

The ceremony so magical in its effects
was undergone this morning at St.
Mildred's Church in the City. Mrs.
G. and G. were both present and appeared to feel no little satisfaction.
Indeed Godwin throughout has shewn
the most polished and cautious attentions to me and Mary.—He seems to
think no kindness too great in com-
pensation for what has past. I confess
I am not entirely deceived by this;
tho' I cannot make my vanity wholly
insensible to certain attentions paid in
a manner studiously flattering.—Mrs.
G. presents herself to me in her real
attributes of affectation prejudice and

heartless pride. Towards her, I confess I never feel an emotion of anything but antipathy. Her sweet daughter is very dear to me.

We left the Hunts yesterday morning, and spent the evening at Skinner-street, not unpleasantly. We had a bed in the neighbourhood and breakfasted with them before the marriage. Very few inquiries have been made of you, and those not of a nature to shew that their suspicions have been alarmed. Indeed, all is safe there.

I write to Clairmont by to-day's post inclosing him £20.—So that you see our expected advantage from added income this quarter comes to very little. Do not answer our letter, as we shall be on our way to you before it can reach London.—The G's give the most singular accounts of Mrs. Boinville, etc.—

I will not tell you how dreadfully melancholy Skinner-street appears with all its associations. The most horrid thought is how people can be merry there! But I am resolved to overcome such sensations. If I do not destroy them I may be myself destroyed.

The Baxters, we hear, have suddenly lost all their fortune, and are reduced to the lowest poverty.

Adieu my dear. Keep up your spirits and manage your health till we come back. It will be Wednesday evening at nine o'clock. Adieu my dear— kiss Willy and yourself for me.

Ever affectionately yours,

P. B. SHELLEY.

Mary can't write being all day with Mrs. Godwin.

[*Addressed outside.*]
    Mrs. Clairmont,
        12 *New Bond Street, Bath.*

LETTER II.

[LONDON :
Postmark—*January* 30*th*, 1817.]

MARY has written to you, dearest Clare, in better spirits, and as a reward of her good spirits, with better news than I.   In fact that about Hunt was overruled.   It only serves to exhibit the malice of these monsters.—

I have little doubt in my own mind but that they will finally succeed in the criminal part of the business.   I mean that some such punishment as imprisonment and fine will be awarded me, by a jury.   But do not disquiet yourself.   Do not allow this to be a matter of present agitation to you.   It is not a thing that can be decided within six months, an interval pregnant with many hopes and fears, and if well cultivated fruitful in joys which might make a bower of roses of the worst dungeon that tyranny could invent. Dont teaze yourself Clarice. The greatest good you can do me is to keep well and quiet yourself, and of that you are well aware.

Mary tells me that she never engaged the lodgings for a month, or that if she did so, one fortnight of the time is already past.

[*Addressed outside.*]
 P. B. Shelley, Esq.,
  12 *New Bond S^t..*
   Bath.

LETTER III.

Mr. Hoppner's,
Friday. [*August*, 1818.]

MY DEAR CLARE,

We arrived at Venice yesterday about five o'clock. Our little girl had shown symptoms of increased weakness and even convulsive motions of the mouth and eyes which made me anxious to see the physician. As she passed from Fusina to the Inn, she became worse. I left her on landing and took a gondola for Dr. Alietti. He was not at home.— When I returned I found Mary in the hall of the inn in the most dreadful distress.

Worse symptoms had appeared. Another Physician had arrived. He told me there was no hope. In about an hour—how shall I tell you—she died—silently, without pain.   And she is now buried.

The Hoppners instantly came and took us to their house—a kindness I should have hesitated to accept, but that this unexpected stroke reduced Mary to a kind of despair.

She is better to day.—

I have sent a message to Albè to say that I cannot see him to day—unless he will call here.   Mary means to try and persuade him to let Allegra stay.

All this is miserable enough—is it not ?—but must be borne—and above all my dear girl take care of yourself.—

Your affectionate Friend,

P. B. S.

[*Addressed outside.*]
   La Signora Clairmont.

LETTER IV.

Friday Mor.

MY BEST AND DEAREST GIRL,

How excessively grieved I am that I have made you share our false alarm ! The whole business merely consists in the omission of the payment of £30 to Hume, and that rascal Longdill having taken out an order against my whole income—a mistake remedied as quickly as known.   I shall send you the money for the ensuing month directly.

Our fright was not small; for we could not conjecture the truth.

Whatever I have or have not however, is dear to me in possession chiefly as an instrument of your peace and independence.

Good-bye dear, yours ever afftely.

S.

[*Addressed outside.*]
   To Miss Clairmont,
      presso al Prof. Bojti,
         Piazza Pitti,
            Firenze.

LETTER V.

[*Postmark:* PISA,
January 10*th*, 1820.]

MY DEAR CLARE

I am seriously distressed to perceive by your letters the vacillating state of your health and spirits : and can only offer you the consolation of unavailing wishes. If they were as effectual as they are sincere your ills would have a very short duration. You do me injustice in imagining that I am in any degree insensible to your pleasure or pain. I wish, since I am so incapable of communicating the one or relieving the other, that I could be so.

I see Emilia sometimes, who always talks of you and laments your absence.

She continues to enchant me infinitely ; and I soothe myself with the idea that I make the discomfort of her cap-

tivity lighter to her by demonstration
of the interest which she has awakened
in me.

I have not been able to see until the
last day or two, or I should have written to you. My eyes are still weak.
I have suffered also considerably from .
my disease ; and am already in imagination preparing to be cut for the stone,
in spite of Vacca's consolatory assur-
ance.

We send you the Papers ; and a
parcel containing your Habit, and
Sintram etc. has been prepared some
days for the Procaccino, who does not
part until to-morrow. You will probably receive that and this letter at
once.

All your wishes have been attended
to respecting *Julian and Maddalo*, which
never was intended for publication.

So it seems that it would have been
better for you to have remained at Pisa.
Yet being now at Florence make the

best profit of your situation : and do not on any account neglect, if possible, to present the letter to the Princess Montemeletto, taking especial care to specify *who* is the writer. You ought to be aware that if this gland should be scrofulous, no small portion of the disease consists in the dejection of spirits and inactivity of mind attached to it ; it is at once a cause and an effect of it, for which the best remedy is society and amusement, and for which even bustle and occupation would be a palliation. Pacchiani is not yet returned.

Farewell my dear girl. Confide in the sincere friendship and unceasing interest of yours affectionately,

S.

[*Addressed outside.*]
　　Miss Clairmont,
　　　　Presso Professore Bojti.
　　　　　　dirimpetto Palazzo Pitti,
　　　　　　　　Firenze.

LETTER VI.

My Dear Clare

Many thanks for your kind and tender letter which Mrs. M. gave me to-day, several days I believe after it had arrived.—I had been very ill, and had not seen her for a fortnight. I had several times been going to write to you, to request you to love me better than you do—when meanwhile your letter arrived. I shall punctually follow all such portions of the advice it contains which are practicable. I write to-night that I may not seem to neglect you, though I have little time : I am delighted to hear of your re-covered health—may I entreat you to be cautious in keeping it. Mine is far better than it has been; and the *relapse* which I now suffer into a state of ease from one of pain, is attended with such an excessive susceptibility of nature, that I suffer equally from pleasure and from pain. You will ask me naturally enough *where I* find any pleasure? The wind, the light, the air, the smell of a flower affects me with violent emotions. There needs no catalogue of the causes of pain.

I see Emily sometimes; and whether her presence is the source of pain or pleasure to me, I am equally ill-fated in both. I am deeply interested in her destiny, and that interest can in no manner influence it. She is not however insensible to my sympathy, and she counts it among her alleviations. As much comfort as she receives from my attachment to her *I lose.*

There is no reason that you should fear any mixture of that which you call *love.* My conception of Emilia's

talents augments every day.   Her
moral nature is fine—but not above
circumstances.   Yet I think her tender and true—which is always something.   How many are only one of
these things at a time !

So much for sentiment and ethics.

The Williams's are come, and Mrs. W.
dined here to-day, an extremely pretty
and gentle woman, apparently not *very*
clever.   I like her very much.   I have
only seen her for an hour, but I will
tell you more another time.   Mary
will write you sheets of gossip.   I
have not seen Mr. W.—

The Greek expedition appears to be
broken up.   No news of any kind that
I know of.

You delight me with your progress
in German, in spite of the reproach
which accompanies the account of it.
Occupy, amuse, instruct, multiply yourself and your faculties—and defy the foul
fiend.   I wish to Heaven, my dear girl,

that *I* could be of any avail to add to your pleasures or diminish your pains —how ardently you cannot know, you only know, as you frequently take care to tell me, how vainly. I can do you no other good than in keeping up the unnatural connexion between this feeble mass of diseases and infirmities and the rapid and weary spirit doomed to drag it through the world.

I took up the pen for an instant only to thank you,—and if you will, to kiss you for your kind attention to me, and I find I have written in ill spirits which may infect you. Let them not do so !—I will write again to-morrow.

Meanwhile your's most tenderly —

S.

[*Addressed outside.*]
    La Sig^a. Clairmont,
        presso al Professore Bojti,
            dirimpetto Palazzo Pitti,
                Firenze.

LETTER VII.

[PISA,

February 17*th*, 1820.]

MY DEAREST FRIEND,

I write in great haste at the Bankers not to lose the Post, and send you a check for two months.—A thousand thanks for your affectionate letter, which to me is as water in the desart. I hope to tell you of Del Rosso by next post, he has just sent for his money which is paid him.

Adieu, best Clare—

Yours ever,

S.

PISA, *Friday.* [*Addressed outside.*]
Miss Clairmont,
presso al Prof. Bojti,
dirimpetto Palazzo Pitti,
Firenze.

LETTER VIII.

Sunday.

My Dearest Friend,

I wrote a line only with the check, which I hope you have received; I had not time on that day to answer your letters.—

Your predilection for Germany, German literature and manners, and for an attempt at forming some connections there, still continues.—There can be no harm in maturing the attempt, should you succeed in finding a fit occasion for it, because you can always recede, in case it should not answer your expectations. The situation of Dame de compagnie is one indeed in which there is little to be hoped compared with what is to be feared; calculating on common cases, but I am willing to believe that yours is an exception to these, and that every one who knows you intimately must find a necessity of interesting themselves deeply in you.—But what are your opportunities, that you so confidently discuss the merits of the question as if the determination of it were in your power? Has the Princess engaged to interest herself in your affairs,—or any other of your acquaintances at Florence? If, indeed, it be in your power to accompany some German Lady of rank to her own country, I think, under the impressions you seem to have conceived, you ought not to delay putting it into effect. It is not as if you had no scheme of life in reserve to which you can retreat.

But you can always reassume your present situation.

—You are indeed Germanizing very fast, and the remark you made of the distinction between the manner in which mind is expressed upon the physiognomy or the entire figure of the Italian or the Austrian is in the choicest style of the *criticism of pure reason.* . . . There is a great deal of truth in it : of truth surrounded and limited by so many exceptions, as entirely to destroy its being, as a practical law of pathognomy.—I hope you will find Germany and the Germans answer your expectations.   I have had no opportunity of forming an idea of them—their Philosophy as far as I understand it, contemplates only the silver side of the shield of truth : better in this respect than the French, which only saw the narrow edge of it.—

You send no news of Naples and Neapolitan affairs; we know nothing of them except what we hear from Florence.   Every post may be expected to bring decisive news, for even the news that they defend themselves against so immense and well appointed a force, is decisive.—I hate the cowardly envy which prompts such base stories as Sgricci's about the Neapolitans : a set of slaves who dare not to imitate the high example of clasping even the shadow of Freedom, alledge the ignorance and excesses of a populace, which oppression has made savage in sentiment and understanding.

That the populace of the city of Naples are brutal, who denies to be taught? they cannot improvise tragedies as Sgricci can, but is it certain that under no excitement they would be incapable of more enthusiasm for their country? Besides it is not of them we speak, but of the people of the Kingdom of Naples, the cultivators of the soil ; whom a sudden and great impulse might awaken into citizens and men, as the French and Spaniards have been awakened, and may render instruments of a system of future social life before which the existing anarchies of Europe will be dissolved and absorbed.—This feeling is base among the Tuscans about Naples.—As to the Austrians I doubt not they are strong men, well disciplined, obeying the master motion like the wheels of a perfect engine : they may even have, as men, more individual excellence and perfection (not that I believe it) than the Neapolitans,—but all these things, if the Spirit of Regeneration is abroad are chaff before the storm, the very elements and events will fight against them, indignation and shameful repulse will burn after them to the vallies of the Alps—Lombardy will renew the league against the Imperial power, which once was so successful, and as the last and greatest consummation, Germany itself will wrest from its oppressors, a power confided to them under stipulations which after having assumed they refused to carry into effect—. . . You have seen or heard, I suppose of the note sent by the British Ministry to the Allied sovereigns. Even the unprincipled Castlereagh dared not join them against Naples, and ventured to condemn the principles of their alliance ; saying as much as to forbid them to touch Spain or Portugal. . . . If the Austrians meet with any serious check—they may as well at once retire, for the good spirit of the World is out against them.—If they march to Naples at once, let us hide our heads in sorrow, for our hopes of political good are vain—

My dearest girl I wish you would contrive some means of causing the Petition of Emilia to be presented to the Grand-duchess. I have engaged that I will procure its presentation, and although perhaps we may conceive little hope from the application there is yet the possibility of success.—She made *me* write the Petition for her, though she could have done it a thousand times better herself; for she has written to the Princess Rospigliosi to entreat her to second the prayer of the petition in a manner that I am persuaded must produce some effect— it is so impressive and pathetic.—The Petition is the very reverse—but these affairs are less determined by words than by facts.—Would Bojti present it? No, that is not good. Could you ask Mad^{e.} Martini to do so, or Mad^{e.} Orlandini? Pray do something for me about this, otherwise I must come to Florence, which does not suit me in any manner.—

Del Rosso I have not yet seen. I was to have gone to Leghorn yesterday, but Williams who is to accompany me, was obliged to stay till to day.—I will write of it from that place.—

What pleasure it gives me to hear that you are well. . . . health is the greatest possession health of body and mind. . . . as the writer, weak enough in both, too well knows.—Tell me particularly how you get on with your Italian friends—study German—I will give you a dictionary if I can find one at Leghorn. " Be strong, live happy and love," says Milton. Adieu dear girl—confide and persuade yourself of my eternal and tender regard.

Yours with deepest affection

S.

Keats is very ill at Naples—I have written to him to ask him to come to Pisa, without however inviting him into our own house. We are not rich enough for that sort of thing. Poor fellow !—I am provoked at Sgricci's assumption, and shall certainly never allow him to make the use you allude to of me.

[*Addressed outside.*]
    Miss Clairmont
        presso al Sig^{e.} Proff^{e.} Bojti.
             dirimpetto Palazzo Pitti
                    Firenze.

[The leaf on which the conclusion of this letter was written had been the rejected commencement of a letter to Keats. On turning it upside down, we can read the cancelled words.]

LETTER IX.

PISA,
Oct. 29*th,* 1820.

MY DEAREST CLARE,

I wrote to you a kind of a scrawl the other day merely to show that I had not forgotten you, and as it was taxed with a postscript by Mary it contained nothing that I wished it to contain. Mrs. Mason has just given me your letter brought by the Tantinis. I called on the Tantinis last night, and am pained to find that they confirm the intelligence of your letter. They tell me you looked very melancholy and disconsolate, which they impute to the weather. You must indeed be very uncomfortable for it to become visible to them. Keep up your spirits my best girl until we meet at Pisa. But for Mrs. Mason, I should say, come back immediately and give up a plan so inconsistent with your feelings—as it is, I fear you had better endure—at least until you come here. You know however, whatever you shall determine on, where to find one ever affectionate Friend, to whom your absence is too painful for your return ever to be unwelcome. I think it moreover for your own interest to observe certain——. As to introductions, believe me I will try my best. I have seen little lately of Mrs. M. nor when one sees her is it easy to nail her attention to what you wish to say, unless you make a direct demand, which in this present case I can hardly do. Medwin's friends are yet to come. I feel almost certain on their arrival of being able to get introductions of some sort or other for you from him. I have not yet spoken to him of it, but I know that he would do all in his power.

I have suffered within this last week a violent access of my disease, with a return of those spasms that I used to have. I am consoled by the persuasion that the seat of the disease is in the kidneys, and consequently not mortal. As to the pain, I care little for it; but the nervous irritability which it leaves is a great and serious evil to me, and which if not incessantly combated by myself and soothed by others would leave me nothing but torment in life.— I am now much better. Medwin's cheerful conversation is of some use to me, but what would it be to your sweet consolation, my own Clare?

We have now removed to a lodging on the Lung Arno, which is sufficiently commodious, and for which we pay thirteen sequins a month. It is next door to that marble palace, and is called Palazzo Galetti, consisting of an excellent mezzanino, and of two rooms on the fourth story, all to the south; and with two fireplaces. The rooms above, one of which is Medwin's room and the other my study (congratulate me on my seclusion) are delightfully pleasant, and to day I shall be employed in arranging my books and gathering my papers about me. Mary has a very good room below, and there is plenty of space for the babe. I expect the water of Pisa to relieve me, if indeed the disease be what is conjectured.

I have read or written nothing lately, having been much occupied by my sufferings, and by Medwin, who relates wonderful and interesting things of the interior of India. We have also been talking of a plan to be accomplished with a friend of his, a man of large fortune, who will be at Leghorn next Spring, and who designs to visit Greece, Syria and Egypt in his own ship. This man has conceived a great admiration for my verses, and wishes above all things that I could be induced to join his expedition. How far all this is practicable, considering the state of my finances I know not yet. I know that if it were it would give me the greatest pleasure, and the pleasure might be either doubled or divided by your presence or absence.

All this will be explained and determined in time ; meanwhile lay to your heart what I say, and do not mention it in your letters to Mary.

The Gisborns are acting as ill as possible about the Steamboat. Mrs. G. wants to apply the engine to their own use, in working a bellows to cast iron : a mere scheme to defraud us. Henry came to the Bagni the other day, and I had a long and very explicit conversation with him, the result of which was that if the affairs which remained of the Steamboat were to be carried on through Mr. G. I absolutely refused

to take any further part in the concern,
except to receive whatever money they
chose to give me as proceeding from
the sale of the materials. At the
same time, should he decide on taking
that side of the alternative, I assured
him that I should take some pains to
acquaint my friends with the bad treat-
ment I had received from him and
his family. The result of the conversation was, that four hundred crowns
were necessary to complete the boat,
and that this sum should be raised
upon the materials of the engine, and
instantly applied to that purpose. I
am in hopes thus, by enlisting their
own interest in the concern, and
showing my resolution to advance no
more money to get it finished ; though
it is true that I risk my interest in the
sale of the materials, which, if Mr.
Gisborn should find some fresh scheme
for preventing the success of the enter-
prise would be all swallowed up in the

debt thus created.   But at all events
I should receive very little from the
sale, and in this manner I may be
repaid the whole.—These Gisbornes are
people totally without faith.—I think
they are altogether the most filthy and
odious animals with which I ever came
in contact.—   They do not visit Mary
as they promised, and indeed if
they did, I certainly should not stay
in the house to receive them.   I
have already planned a retreat to
Mrs. Mason's.—

I am going to study Arabic—for a
purpose and a motive as you may
conceive.—I wish you would enquire
for me at Florence whether there are
an Arabic Grammar and Dictionary,
and any other Arabic books, either
printed or Manuscript, to be bought.
You can first ask Dr. Bojti, and if he
knows nothing, go to Molini's library
and enquire of him.   At all events go
to Molini's and send me all the in-

formation you can pick up. I trust this to your kind love.

If I buy and pay for any I can send you your scudi at the same time which I have made some ineffectual efforts to convey to Florence. Pardon me my dearest for mentioning scudi, and do not love me less because they are a portion of the inevitable dross of life, which clings to our friendship.—

Your most affectionate
SHELLEY.

[*Addressed outside.*]
  La Signora Clairmont
    per ricapito al Professore Bojti
      Piazza dei Pitti
        Firenze.

LETTER X.

CASA GALETTI, PISA,
November, Wednesday,
[1820]

MY DEAR CLARE,

Something indeed must be instantly decided respecting your present situation—unfit in every respect for you, and fraught with consequences to your health and spirits which I cannot endure to think of. I had spoken to Mrs. Mason of it, and her reply was that *when you return from Pisa to Florence*, she will give you a letter to the Princess, charging me at the same time to keep this promise a secret from you ; for what motive I cannot divine. I have not done so, you see,—and indeed I could not, without urging your immediate return. The great thing now is, if possible, to come to Pisa before you shall stand engaged for another month, or perhaps another three months—for such was the arrangement decided upon at Florence. Could you not make some excuse for preceding them to Pisa? Or still better, could you not do it without assigning any reason, and then determine with me and Mrs. Mason upon what should be done on their arrival? This must be done, or you stand pledged for some indefinite time.

The only consideration to make you hesitate, *is* how far such a step would offend Mrs. Mason—that is, how far it would affect any future aid you might derive from her. Poor Mrs. M. is now very ill, slowly convalescing from a dangerous colic; she cannot bear the light, or the air, or the least motion. You may judge, she is [in] no state to permit me to agitate this question. Before her illness, when I talked to her, she seemed to think it weak and unreasonable in you, not to bear all this

solitude and inconvenience in the hope
of some change, or something that she
could or would do.—She opposed
strongly the idea of your return ; and it
was on that occasion that she spoke of
the Princess Montemilitto ;—which
introduction, if it could be carried into
effect, would certainly place you in a
situation to require no other.   But as
she has not seen or heard from the
Princess for sixteen years, we cannot be
sure of the reception her recommenda-
tion would meet. Everything however
consists in the manner—and I by no
means recommend you to freeze or
mope yourself to death on the chance
of this Princess.—I would advise,
contriving by some form of words, to
part from your hosts on the best possible
terms, and with a mutual understanding
that the connexion was to be renewed
again, so soon as you had fulfilled the
object of your leaving them.—Leave
some sort of opening, but just so small

as that they should not be able without further communication to hold you liable on the 20th for three additional months.

It is great pity that the day of their arrival at Pisa, exceeds the month, or it might all have admitted of a far simpler mode of arrangement. I don't think Mrs. Mason could be seriously angry—I am sure she would have no reason—nor do I think that it would make any difference in her giving you an introduction to the Princess. The only care need be, that it should be so managed as not, at least for the present, to offend or alarm the Bojtis, and that you tell Mrs. Mason, that you determined to employ the interval of the few days that remained of the month, in taking her advice respecting how far a further residence with them could be made available to your purposes. And that you were determined (as I think you right to determine) not to make a three months additional engagement to spend the winter in the frore climate of Florence, merely to suffer. My advice therefore is, that you take a place in the Diligence and return here instantly, without offending or alarming the Bojtis. You cannot hesitate without making yourself liable for an engagement of three additional months, and I am persuaded that Mrs. Mason is too reasonable and too good not to feel that this step is completely justifiable by the alternative in which you stand, of either taking it, or engaging in a longer term—in which unless some alteration takes place you expend health and spirits for no imaginable purpose.—This step pledges you to nothing,—and after painful and serious consideration of the circumstances of your situation it is my deliberate advice. Read this letter over twice or three times, before you decide to act, and completely understand what you are about.

We are at Casa Galetti, next door to that marble palace with Alla Giornata written on it.—

There is yet no letter from Ravenna— a delay which you cannot from experience think extraordinary.

I do not send you the Papers; because I do not see how you can do otherwise than come.—Let me repeat it again—do not part on bad or even on indifferent terms with the Bojtis. All depends on that—and it is so easy to say that some one is ill, if you think it necessary to make any express explanation.—

It rains incessantly, but the climate is exceedingly mild, and we have no fires. How sorry I am, my poor girl, to hear that your glands are bad.— You must take care of yourself this winter, and eat nourishing food, and try and deceive care. How I long to see you again, and take what care I can of you—but do not imagine that if I did not most seriously think it best for you that I would advise you to return.   I have suffered horribly from my side, but my general health decidedly improves, and there is now no doubt but that it is a disease of the kidneys which, however it sometimes makes life intolerable, has, Vacca assures me, no tendency to endanger it.   May it be prolonged that I may be the source of whatever consolation or happiness you are capable of receiving !

Mary is well, and the babe brilliantly well, and very good—he scarcely suffers at all from his teeth.

Medwin is very agreeable—I do not know him well enough to say that he is amiable.   He plays at chess, and falls into our habits of reading in the evening, and Mary likes him well enough.—Henry Revely has been frequently at Pisa, and always dines with us, in spite of a conversation which I had with him, and which was

intended to put an end to all intercourse
between me and that base family.—I
have not the heart to put my interdict
in effect upon Henry,—he is so very
miserable, and such a whipped and
trembling dog. You have no conception
of the stories that he tells about
the Riccis.   There is no decisive news
yet from London about the Queen—it
is expected this day, and all the papers
of the trial have been kept for you.—
Adieu, dearest—be careful to tear this
letter to pieces as I have written
(carelessly ?)

Yours faithfully,

S.

This only bit of paper I have is the
beginning of a letter addressed to
Henry*—never mind it.

I am happy that the *Hyperion* and
the *Prometheus* please you. My verses

* The leaf on which the conclusion of this letter was
written had been the rejected commencement of a letter
to Henry Revely.   The six lines of which the cancelled
fragment consists are quite legible.

please so few persons that I make much of the encouragement of the few, whose judgement (if I were to listen to Vanity, the familiar spirit of our race) I should say with Shakespeare and Plato "outweighed a whole theatre of others."

[*Addressed outside.*]
　　　　Miss Clairmont,
　　　　　presso al Prof. Bojti,
　　　　　　dirimpetto Palazzo Pitti,
　　　　　　　　Firenze.

LETTER XI.

'Οψιλάντι   [Pisa,
                           April 2nd, 1821.]
           [*Written by Mary.*]
My Dear Claire,

Greece has declared its freedom! Prince Mavrocordato had made us expect this event for some weeks past. Yesterday he came *rayonnant de joie*— he had been ill for some days but he forgot all his pains. Ipselanti, a Greek general in the service of Russia, has collected together 10,000 Greeks and entered Wallachia, declaring the liberty of his country. The Morea—Epirus— Servia are in revolt. Greece will most certainly be free. The worst part of this news for us is that our amiable prince will leave us—he will of course join his countrymen as soon as possible —never did man appear so happy—yet

he sacrifices family—fortune—everything
to the hope of freeing his country.
Such men are repaid—such succeed.
You may conceive the deep sympathy
that we feel in his joy on this occasion :
tinged as it must be with anxiety for
success—made serious by the knowledge
of the blood that must be shed on this
occasion.   What a delight it will be to
visit Greece free.

April has opened with a weather
truly heavenly—after a whole week of
libeccio—rain and wind, it is delightful
to enjoy one of these days peculiar to
Italy in this early season—the clear
sky, animating sun and fresh yet not
cold breeze—just that delicious season
when pleasant thoughts bring sad ones
to the mind, when every sensation
seems to make a double effect and
every moment of the day is divided
felt and counted.   One is not gay—at
least I am not—but peaceful and at
peace with all the world.

I write you a short letter to day but I could not resist the temptation of acquainting you with the changes in Greece the moment Prince Mavrocordato gave us leave to mention it.

I hope that your spirits will get better with this favourable change of weather— Florence must be perfectly delightful. Send the white paint as soon as you can and two *strisce's* for me. Shelley says that he will finish this letter—We hear from no one in England.

Ever yours,
M. W. S.

[*Continued by Shelley.*]

MY DEAR FRIEND,

I hope you have somewhat recovered your spirits, since you last wrote to me ; if so, pray tell me, as it makes me very melancholy to hear that you are so much depressed. The weather is a medicine for almost any dejection which does not spring from a naturally imperfect or deranged frame. My health is very fluctuating and uncertain — and change of season brings a change rather than a relief of ills. I live however for certain intercalary moments which are the "ounces of sweet that outweigh a pound of sour," and which no person deprived of memory need despair of possessing.

Tell me, what do you mean to do on the 20th and how are your prospects with the Princess? Naples will be no place to visit at present and you are much deceived by those who surround you, if you imagine that the success of the Austrians in that country has terminated the war in Italy. *We* are yet undecided for the summer—say something to fix our determination. The Catholic Emancipation has passed the second reading by a majority of 11 on 497. This will give the Government a momentary strength. Pray order Calderon for me without delay·

and try if you can urge the bookseller
to some sort of speed.—

Pray don't imagine that the trees
upon the letter you sent to Mary are my
manufacture—I disclaim such daubs—
and I had hoped that you knew my style
too well to impute them to me. The
love-letters themselves do not seem to
have been meant for you. Is there
no other Clara Clairmont in the world
but the one to whom I declare myself
the constant and affectionate friend,

S.

[Tree-tops roughly sketched.]
    That is my style.

[*Addressed outside.*]
    Miss Clairmont,
        presso al Prof. Bojti,
            dirimpetto Palazzo Pitti,
                Firenze.

LETTER XII.

.[*Postmark:* PISA ;
May, 1821.]

MY DEAREST CLARE,

It is not for want of interest in your plans and feelings, that I have not written to you : but, imagining that Mary managed the *rude stuff,* the mass, of the correspondence ; and not knowing that I had anything peculiar to say to you, I had kept the silence of one to whom letters and indeed communication of any kind, is either a great bain or a great pleasure.—So far have I been from neglecting you in my thoughts, that I have lately had with Mrs. Mason long and serious conversations respecting your situation and prospects : conversations too long, too important, and embracing too various a complication of views to detail in a letter.—You can perhaps guess at some of them.—I am most anxious to know your expectations and determinations, at Florence. Whatever these may be, either there or elsewhere, believe that no view which I can take of any plan you may determine on, will be influenced by anything else than a consideration of *your own* ultimate advantage. I feel, my dear girl, that in case the failure of your expectations at Florence should induce you to think of other plans, *we*, that is you and I ought to have a conversation together.

My health is in general much the same : somewhat amended by the divine weather that has fallen upon us, but still characterized by irritability and depression ; or moments of almost supernatural elevation of spirits. My side begins however to feel the influence of the relaxing year. I think I have been better altogether this winter; I wish to think so, in spite of the strong motives which should impel me to desire to exist under another form.— I have bought a boat, which Williams overturned the first evening by taking hold of the top of the mast ;—as you might any boat under a sloop of war. I expect that the exercise of sailing etc. will do good to my health : I have bought it instead of a horse, which Vaccà recommended ; but which would cost more money, spirits, time, trouble, and care than I have to expend conveniently.   Henry Reveley has got her now at Leghorn to paint and refit ; and she will be a very nice little shell, for the Nautilus your friend . . . who, has enough to do in taming his own will, without the additional burthen of regulating that of a horse, and still worse, of a groom.—The Gisborns are going to England. They have been here for two days on a visit, proposed by themselves, and return tomorrow. My manners to them have been gentle,

but cold.   Not a word of the Steam
Boat—in fact my money seems to be
as irretrievable as Henry's character,
and it is fortunate that I value it as
little.——I do not write anything at
present.   I feel incapable of composition.

I believe it is now certain that Emilia
will marry, although it is undecided
whom.—A great and a painful weight
will be taken off my mind by that
event.   Poor thing! she suffers dreadfully in her prison.

Adieu.   Your affectionate friend,

S.

I Mantuan, capering, squalid, squalling.
A verse of Mr. T[aaffe]'s translation of
Dante.

[*Addressed outside.*]
    Miss Clairmont,
        Presso al Prof^{e.} Bojti,
            dirimpetto Palazzo Pitti,
                Firenze.

LETTER XIII.

PISA,
June 8th, 1821.

MY DEAR CLARE,

I have just seen Mrs. Mason, who desires me on your part not to take further steps about your lodgings at Livorno: I accordingly stay all proceedings until further orders.—Indeed you would be very uncomfortable there alone, or in the society of those odious people, the dregs of the Livornese merchants, who sell board and lodging on such terms as are by no means large enough to include the increased appetite that sea-bathing would give you. If you can go with Madam Orlandini pray do. The Gisborns I told you are going to England and are selling all their goods, and mine too. I wonder how much they will have the face to offer me as the produce of the wreck of the steamboat. We shall see. I shall pounce upon their German dictionary for you; as the order I transmitted to Peacock for one, has been like all my other orders, totally neglected. My health is better since I last wrote. I always tell you it is better, and yet I am never well. I have a great desire and interest to live, and I would submit to any inconvenience to attain that object. I take all sorts of care of myself, but it *appears* to make no difference. Anything that prevents me from thinking does me good. Reading does not occupy me enough: the only relief I find springs from the composition of poetry, which necessitates contemplations that lift me above the stormy mist of sensations which are my habitual place of abode. I have lately been composing a poem on Keats: it is better than anything that I have yet written, and worthy both of him and of me.

We never hear from England now. Godwin writes no more.

Peacock writes no more. Hunt wrote about three months ago, in a strain however which gave me pain, because I see he is struggling. Miss Curran wrote the other day inviting herself to spend the summer with us ; but Mary sent an excuse. We see a good deal of the Williams's, who are very good people, and I like her much better than I did. Mr. Taaffe comes sometimes, and on an occasion of sending two guinea pigs to Mary wrote this at the end of his letter:

" O, that I were one of those guinea pigs, that I might see you this morning " !—

A vessel has arrived to take the Greek Prince and his suite to join the army in the Morea. He is a great loss to Mary and *therefore* to me. . but not otherwise.

Adieu. I will send you the rest of your money in a day or two.

Ever truly and affectionately your's

S.

P.S.—Untreue trifft seinen eigenen Herrn.

[*Addressed outside.*]

Miss Clairmont,

Presso al Prof. Bojti,

dirimpetto Palazzo Pitti,

Firenze.

LETTER XIV.

Pisa, *Saturday.*
[*Postmark: June 19th, 1821.*]

MY DEAREST CLARE

Have you made your mind up where you would live this summer? or is there anything new in your plans? I hear from you but seldom now you cease to correspond with Mary.

Horace Smith is coming out to Italy immediately. He requests me to discover for him in or near Florence, an house fit for a very small establishment, with a garden, large enough for a family in all of seven or eight persons.— He wishes also to get an *Italian woman, good cook, who speaks French.* This last I apprehend to be impossible. You know how much I wish to do my utmost in executing all Horace Smith's commissions: and I thought of coming to Florence, though it would be a great waste both of money and of health to me, for that purpose.   But perhaps you could manage these affairs ; of course the house will not be taken until he comes, and will be subject to his approbation.   I imagine he wishes it to be unfurnished, and he is the sort of man to like a pretty, elegant, neat, well-kept little place.

Let me see if I have any news for you.   I have received a most melancholy account of the last illness of poor Keats, which I will neither tell you nor send you ; for it would make you too low-spirited.—My elegy on him is finished : I have dipped my pen in consuming fire to chastise his destroyers ; otherwise the tone of the poem is solemn and exalted.—I send it to the press here, and you will soon have a copy.—

Horace Smith tells me a curious circumstance, which if I were in England, would work me much annoyance. A low bookseller has got hold of *Queen Mab*, and published it, and says he will defy all prosecutions, and is selling them by thousands.

Horace Smith applied for an injunction on my part, but, like Southey in *Wat Tyler*, was refused. The abuse which all the Government prints are pouring forth on me, and, as H. S. says, the "diabolical calumnies which they vent, and which religion alone could inspire," is boundless.—I enjoy and am amused with the turmoil of these poor people ; but perhaps it is well for me that the Alps and the Ocean are between us.—Medwin is going to be married to a daughter of Sir E. Dalbyn only 15 years old. He is in full chase to Venice.—I am trying to persuade Mary to ask your pardon,— I hope that I shall succeed.—In the meantime, as you were in the wrong you had better not ask hers, for that is unnecessary, but write to her—if you had been in the right you would have done so.—

Emilia's Marriage is put off to September. I think of spending next winter at Florence. Mary talks of Rome.—We see the Williams constantly—nice, goodnatured people, very soft society after authors and pretenders to philosophy. Godwin's *Malthus* is come: a dry but clever book, with decent interspersions of cant and sophistry.

Dearest girl—your most affectionate Friend.—

P. B. S.—

I don't send your money till I hear do you come or no. Write next post.

[*Addressed outside.*]
 Miss Clairmont,
  Presso al Prof^{e.} Bojti,
   Palazzo Pitti,
    Firenze.

LETTER XV.

PISA,
Dec. 11, 1821.

MY DEAREST FRIEND,

I SHOULD be very glad to receive a confidential letter from you—one totally the reverse of those I write to you ; detailing all your present occupation and intimacies, and giving me some insight into your future plans. Do not think that my affection and anxiety for you ever cease, or that I ever love you less although that love has been and still must be a source of disquietude to me.

The Exotic as you please to call me droops in this frost—a frost both moral and physical—a solitude of the heart. These last days I have been unable to ride, the cold towards sunset is so excessive and my side reminding me that I am mortal. Medwin rides almost constantly with Lord B. ; and the party sometimes consists of Gamba, Taaffe, Medwin and the Exotic who unfortunately belonging to the order of mimosa, thrives ill in so large a society. I cannot endure the company of many persons, and the society of one is either great pleasure or great pain.

We expect the Hunts every day, but I suppose the tramontana is a Greek wind at Sea and detains them. I think I told you they were to live at Lord B's.

The news of the Greeks continues to be more and more glorious. It may be said that the Peloponnesus is entirely free, and that Mavrocordato has been acting a distinguished part, and will probably fill a high rank in the magistracy of the infant republic.

What are you doing in German ? I have read none since we met, nor probably until we meet again—should that ever be— shall I read it.

I am employed in nothing—I read— but I have no spirits for serious com- position—I have no confidence, and to write in solitude or put forth :thoughts without sympathy is unprofitable vanity.

Tell me dearest what you mean to do, and if it should give you pleasure come and live with us. The Williamses always speak of you with praise and affection, and regret very much that you did not spend this winter with them, but neither their regret nor their affection equal mine. Yours ever.

S.

[*Addressed outside.*]
   Miss Clairmont
      Presso al Prof. Bojti
         Dirempetto Palazzo Pitti
           Firenze.

LETTER XVI.

December 31, PISA—
[Postmark : 1 *January*, (1822.)]

My Dearest Friend

I returned from Leghorn on Friday evening, but too late for the Post or you should have heard from me. The expected person had not arrived, having been detained by the tremendous weather. I hope soon to have more satisfactory intelligence. Your desires on this subject are the object of my anxious thought.—

Mary desires me to say (not that she sees this letter or any of yours addressed to me) that she should have written to you—but she has been very unwell. She has suffered dreadfully from rheumatism in her head, to such a degree as for some successive nights entirely to deprive her of sleep. She is now, by dint of blisters and laudanum somewhat better. I have ~ suffered considerably from pain, and depression of spirits. The weather has been frightful here. Torrents of rain have swollen the Arno to a greater degree than has been known for many years; the fury of the torrent is inconceivably great. The wind was beyond anything I ever remember, and all the shores of the Mediterranean are strewn with wrecks. The damage sustained at Genoa and the number of lives lost has been immense: the ships suspected of pestilence have been driven from their moorings into the town, and everything coming from Genoa has been subjected to a strict quarantine. Three mails from France are due, and a thousand contradictory rumours are afloat as to the cause. You may imagine, and I am sure you will share our anxiety about poor

Hunt. I wonder, and am shocked at my own insensibility, that I can sleep or· enjoy one moment of peace until I hear of his safety. I shall of course write to tell you the moment of his arrival—I know you will be anxious about these poor people. The ship in which they sailed was spoken with in the Bay of Biscay, and was then quite safe.—We have little new in politics. You will have heard of the amphibious state of things in France, and the establishment of the Ultra-Ministry by the preponderance afforded to that party by the coalition of the Liberals with it.—The Greeks are going on excellently, and those massacres at Smyrna and Constantinople import nothing to the stability of the cause. There is no such thing as a rebellion in Ireland, or anything that looks like it. The people are indeed stung to madness by the oppression of the Irish system, and there is no such thing as getting rents or taxes even at the point of the bayonet throughout the southern provinces. But there are no regular bodies of men in opposition to the Government, nor have the people any leaders. In England all bear for the moment the aspect of a sleeping volcano.

You do not tell me, my dearest Claire, anything of your plans, although you bid me be secret with respect to them. Assure yourself, my best friend, that anything you *seriously* enjoin me, that may be necessary for your happiness will be strictly observed by me. Write to me more explicitly your projects and expectations—you know in some respects my sentiments both with regard to them and you. I have been once, after enduring much solicitation, to Mrs. Beauclerk's, who did me the favour to caress me exceedingly. Unless she calls on Mary I shall not repeat my visit. Do you know her?

Should you take it into your head to call on Molini for me, let not Calderon having been sent for be an objection. —I want a Calderon.

Adieu.   Ever most faithfully yours,

S.

Mrs. Mason told me to say that she does not write because I do.

[*Addressed outside.*]
  Miss Clairmont,
    Presso al Prof. Bojti,
      dirimpetto Palazzo Pitti,
        Firenze.

LETTER XVII.

[*Begun by Mary.*]

[*Italy*, 1822.]

MY DEAR CLAIRE

Shelley and I have been consulting seriously about your letter received this morning, and I wish in as orderly a manner as possible to give you the result of our reflections.   First as to our coming to Florence ; I mentioned it to you first, it is true, but we have so little money, and our calls this quarter for removing &c. will be so great that we had entirely given up the idea.   If it would be of great utility to you, as a single expence we might do it—but if it be necessary that others should follow, the crowns would be minus.   But before I proceed further on this part of the subject let me examine what your plans appear to be.   Your anxiety for A's health is to a great degree unfounded ; Venice, its stinking canals and dirty streets, is enough to kill any child ; but you ought to know, and any one will tell you so, that the towns of Romagna, situated where Bagna-cavallo is, enjoy the best air in Italy—Imola and the neighbouring *paese* are famous. Bagna-callo especially, being 15 miles from the sea and situated on an eminence is peculiarly salutary. Considering the affair reasonably A. is well taken care of there, she is in good health, and in all probability will continue so.

No one can more entirely agree with you than I in thinking that as soon as possible A. ought to be taken out of the hands of one as remorseless as he is unprincipled. But at the same time it appears to me that the present moment is exactly the one in which this is the most difficult—time cannot add to these difficulties for they can

never be greater. Allow me to en-
umerate some of those which are
peculiar to the present instant. A. is
in a convent, where it is next to impossible to get her out ; high walls and
bolted doors enclose her—and more
than all the regular habits of a convent,
which never permits her to get outside
its gates and would cause her to be
missed directly. But you may have a
plan for this and I pass to other ob-
jections. At your desire Shelley urged
her removal to L.B. and this appears
in the highest degree to have exasperated him—he vowed that if you annoyed
him he would place A. in some secret
convent, he declared that you should
have nothing to do with her, and that
he would move heaven and earth to
prevent your interference. L. B. is at
present a man of 12 or 15 thousand a
year, he is on the spot, a man reckless
of the ill he does others, obstinate to
desperation in the pursuance of his

plans or his revenge. What then would you do having A. on the outside of the convent walls? Would you go to America? the money we have not, nor does this seem to be your idea. You probably wish to secrete yourself. But L. B. would use any means to find you out—and the story he might make up—a man stared at by the grand duke—with money at command—and above all on the spot to put energy into every pursuit, would he not find you? If he did not he comes upon Shelley—he taxes him; Shelley must either own it or tell a lie—in either case he is open to be called upon by L. B. to answer for his conduct—and a duel —I need not enter upon that topic, your own imagination may fill up the picture.

On the contrary a little time, a very little time, may alter much of this. It is more than probable that he will be obliged to go to England within a year

—then at a distance he is no longer so formitable [*sic*] what is certain is that we shall not be so near him another year—he may be reconciled with his wife, and though he may bluster he may not be sorry to get A. off his hands ; at any rate if we leave him perfectly quiet he will not be so exasperated, so much on the *qui vive* as he is at present—Nothing remains constant, something may happen— things cannot be worse.   Another thing I mention which though sufficiently ridiculous may have some weight with you.   Spring is our unlucky season. No spring has passed for us without some piece of ill luck.   Remember the first spring at Mrs. Harbottles. The second when you became acquainted with L. B. the third we went to Marlow—no wise thing at least— the fourth our uncomfortable residence in London — the fifth our Roman misery—the sixth Paolo at Pisa — the seventh a mixture of Emilia and a Chancery suit—now the aspect of the Autumnal Heavens has on the contrary been with few exceptions, favourable to us—What think you of this? It is in your own style, but it has often struck me. Would it not be better therefore to wait, and to undertake no plan until circumstance bend a little more to us.

Then we are drearily behind hand with money at present—Hunt and our furniture has swallowed up more than our savings. You say great sacrifices will be required of us, I would make many to extricate all belonging to me from the hands of L. B., whose hypocrisy and cruelty rouse one's soul from its depths. We are of course still in great uncertainty as to our summer residence — we have calculated the great expence of removing our furniture for a few months as far as Spezia, and it appears to us a bad plan—to get a

furnished house we must go nearer
Geneva, probably nearer L. B., which
is contrary to our most earnest wishes.
We have thought of Naples,* in such an
event—Your setting up a school precisely
on Miss Field's plan I certainly never
approved; because I thought even in
Miss Field's case, the prices and the
whole plan ridiculously narrow: and
the whole affair seemed planned on that
plausible scheme of moderation which
never succeeds. It was this that I
wanted to say to you. But the idea of
a school, especially under Mrs. Mason's
protection, I confess appeared very
plausible to me. I should be glad, in
case of transmigration, to leave you
under such powerful and such secure
protection as her's: it would be one
subject less for regret, to me, if I could
consider—my death—as no immediate
misfortune to you; as in this case it

* This letter is written in Mary Shelley's autograph
as far as the word *Naples*, and from *in such an event*
to the end it is in the autograph of Shelley.

would not.—The incumbent of my re-
version still flourishes ; and, you must be
aware that the sensations with which it
has pleased the Devil to endow the
frame of his successor, are not the
strongest pledges of longevity. You
say that I may not have a conversation
with you because you may depart in a
hurry Heaven knows where—Except it
be to the other world (and I know the
coachman of that road will not let the
passengers wait a minute) I know of no
mortal business that requires such post
haste.

We are now at the Baths in a very
nice house looking to the mountains.
Mary will tell you all about it. Little
Babe is quite well, smiling and good.
I am better to day. I have been very
ill, body and soul, but principally the
latter.—I took some exercise in the
boat to dissipate thought : but it
over-fatigued me and made me worse.
The Baths, I think, do me good, but

especially solitude, and not seeing polite human faces, and hearing voices. I go over about twice a week to see Emilia, who is in better spirits and health than she has been for some time.—Danielli almost frightens her to death, and she handed him over to me to quiet and console. — It seems that I am worthy of taking my degree of M.A. in the art of Love, for I have contrived to calm the despairing swain, much to the satisfaction of poor Emilia : who in that convent of hers sees everything as through a mist, ten times its natural size. — The Williams's come sometimes : they have taken Pagnano. W. I like, and I have got reconciled to Jane.—Mr. Taaffe rides, writes, invites, complains, bows and apologizes ; he would be a mortal bore if he came often. The Greek Prince* comes sometimes, and I

*Prince Alexander Mavrocordato.

reproach my own savage disposition that so agre[e]able, accomplished and amiable a person is not more agre[e]able to me.

Adieu, my dear Clare.

Ever yours most affectionately

S.

[*Addressed outside.*]
A Mademoiselle
Mad^{lle} de Clairmont
Chez M. le Professeur Bojti
Florence.

LETTER XVIII.

[Postmark, *March* 20.]

PISA,
Sunday Mor[*ning*, 1822.]

MY DEAR CLARE,

I know not what to think of the state of your mind, or what to fear for you.   Your late plan about Allegra seems to me in its present form pregnant with irremediable infamy to all the actors in it except yourself;— in any form wherein *I* must actively co-operate, with inevitable destruction. I *would not* in any case make myself the party to a forged letter. I *could not* refuse Lord Byron's challenge, though that, however to be deprecated, would be the least in the series of mischiefs consequent upon my pestilent intervention in such a plan.   I say this because I am shocked at the thoughtless violence of your designs, and I wish to put my sense of this madness in the strongest light. I may console myself however with the reflection that the attempt even is impossible ; as I have no money. So far from being ready to lend me 3 or 400 pounds, Horace Smith has lately declined to advance 6 or 7 Napoleons for a musical instrument which I wished to buy for Jane at Paris : nor have I any other Friend to whom I could apply.

You think of going to Vienna. The change might have a favorable effect upon your mind, and the occupation and exertion of a new state of life wean you from counsils so desperate as those to which you have been so lately led. I must try to manage the money for your journey, if so you have decided. You know how different my own ideas are of life. I also have been struck

by the heaviest inflictions almost,
which a high spirit and a feeling heart
ever endured.—Some of yours and of
my evils are in common, and I am
therefore, in a certain degree, a judge.
If you would take my advice you
would give up this idle pursuit after
shadows, and temper yourself to the
season, and seek in the daily and
affectionate intercourse of friends a
respite from these perpetual and
irritating projects. Live from day to
day, attend to your health, cultivate
literature and liberal ideas to a certain
extent, and expect that from time and
change which no exertion of your own
can give you. Serious and calm reflection
has convinced me that you can never
obtain Allegra by such means as you
have lately devised, or by any means
to be devised. Lord Byron is inflexible,
and he has her in his power. Remember Clare when you rejected my earnest
advice at Milan, and how vain is now

your regret !—This is the second of my
Sybilline volumes ; if you wait for the
third it may be sold at a still higher
price. If you think well, this summer,
go to Vienna ; but wherever you go or
stay let the *past* be past.

I expect soon to write to you on
another subject, respecting which, however, all is as you already know.
Farewell. Your affte.

S.

I am much pleased with your translation of *Goethe*, which cannot fail to
succeed if finished as begun. Lord B.
thinks I have sent it to Paris to be
translated, and therefore does not yet
expect a copy. I shall of course have
it copied out for him, and preserve
yours to be sent to England.

I send you 50 Francesconi—6 more
than your income, as you have made
some expenses for me and Mary, I
know not what.— Pray acknowledge
the receipt of it.

Mary has written, she tells me, an account of yesterday's affray. The man, I am sorry to say, is much worse ; but never did any one provoke his own fate so wantonly. I was struck from my horse, and had not Captain Hay warded off the sabre with his stick, I must inevitably have been killed. Captain Hay has a severe sabre wound across the face.

[*Addressed outside.*]
    Miss Clairmont,
        presso al Prof. Bojti,
            Piazza Pitti,
                Firenze.

LETTER XIX.

[PISA, 1822.]

It is of vital importance both to me and to yourself; to Allegra even that I should put a period to my intimacy with L.B. and that without eclat. No sentiments of honour or justice restrain him (as I strongly suspect) from the basest insinuations, and the only mode in which I could effectually silence him; I am reluctant (even if I had proof) to employ during my father's life. But for your immediate feelings I would suddenly and irrevocably leave the country which he inhabits, nor ever enter it but as an enemy to determine our differences *without words.* But at all events I shall soon see you, and then we will weigh both your plans and mine. Write by next post.

[P. B. S.]

LETTER XX.

Lerici,
Tuesday Evening, March 29, 1822.

My Dear Clare,

Tell me when we are to expect you, and the precise hour and day at which you arrive at Viareggio.—I do not expect that you will have found any motives at Florence for altering your intentions with respect to this summer, and I think that at least for the present you would be happier here than anywhere else.   I have heard from Mrs. Mason.   Mary still continues to suffer terribly from languor and hysterical affections; and things in every respect remain as they were when you left us . . . . . The letters on the sail, after having undergone a thousand processes remain still distinct, and the only difference is that the sail is in a dismal condition.—We cannot match the stuff.

I sailed to Massa the other day, and returned late at night against a high sea and heavy wind in which the boat behaved excellently.—I sit within the whole morning and in the evening we sail about.—I write a little—I read and enjoy for the first time these ten years something like health——I find however that I must neither think or feel, or the pain returns to its old nest.

Williams seems happy and content and we enjoy each other's society. Jane is by no means so acquiescent in the system of things, and she pines after her own house and saucepans to which no one can have a claim except herself. It is a pity that one so pretty and amiable should be so selfish — But dont tell her this—and come soon yourself, I hope my best Clare, with

tranquillized spirits and a settled mind
to your ever constant and

affectionate friend,

P. B. S.

Mrs. M. will tell you all Sk. st. news—
—Mary is not in a state to hear it.

[*Addressed outside.*]
   Miss Clairmont,
      presso al Prof. Bojti,
         Piazza Pitti,
            Firenze.

LETTER XXI.

Sunday Evening—
[*Postmark Pisa 2 April*, (1822).]

MY DEAREST FRIEND—

I wish you could in some degree tranquillize yourself, and fix upon some quiet plan of thought and action. The best would probably be to think and act without a plan, and let the world pass. . . No exertions of yours can obtain Allegra, and believe me that the plans you have lately dreamed, would, were they ATTEMPTED only, plunge you and all that is connected with you in irremediable ruin.—But I dare say you are by this time convinced of it.—

One thing I beg you to answer me :

How is your Health? If you have any returns of that affection of the glands of the breasts, you must promise me to see Vaccà.—I am positive and most anxious on this subject,—for ill-health is one of the evils that is not a dream, and the reality of which every year, if you neglect it, will make more impressive.—

This late affair about the Soldier will probably have no consequences. The man is getting better : my part in the affair, if not cautious or prudent, was justifiable : nor can I take to myself any imputation of rashness or want of temper. My words and my actions were calm and peaceable though firm. The fault of the affair, if there be any began with Taaffe, who loudly and impetuously asked Lord Byron if he would submit to the insult offered by the Dragoon. Lord B. might indeed have told Taaffe to redress his own wrongs; but I, who had the swiftest horse, could not have allowed the man to escape, when once the pursuit was begun :—the man was probably drunk . . . Don't be so ready to blame. Imagine that there may be some more temper and prudence in the world, be sides what that little person of yours contains. . . .

Your translation of Göthe is ex- cellent.—I did not understand from you that your name was to be told to Lord B— and I must now adhere to the story already told. I am sure you will gain a great deal by it— if you go on as you have begun— How many pages of the original are done ?

Mary will talk gossip, and send you the Indian air, either by this post or the next.—After a long truce, my side has declared war against me ; and I suppose I must wait for the general paci- fication between me and my rebel faculties before it will be quiet for good.

Ever your affectionate

S—

[*Addressed outside.*]
 Miss Clairmont,
  presso al Sig^{re}. P^e. Bojti,
   Piazza Pitti,
    Firenze.

LETTER XXII.

[PISA, 1822.]

I have little to add to Mary's letter
my poor dear friend—and all that I
shall do is suspend my journey to take
a house until your answer :—Of course,
if you do not spend the summer with
us I shall come to Florence and see
and talk with you.—But it seems to
me far better, on every account that
you should resolve on this and tranquillize yourself among your friends.
I shall certainly take our house *far*
from Lord Byron's, although it may be
impossible suddenly to put an end to
his detested intimacy.—*My* coming to
Florence would cost 15 or 20 crowns ;
Mary's much more : and if therefore
we. are to see you soon this money

in our present situation were better spared.—

Mary tells you that Lord Byron is obstinate and *awake* about Allegra; my great object had been to lull him into security until circumstances might call him to England. But the idea of contending with him in Italy and defended by his enormous fortune is vain.—I was endeavouring to induce him to place Allegra in the institute at Lucca, but his jealousy of my regard for *your* interests will, since a conversation I had with him the other day, render him inaccessible to my suggestions.—It seems to me, that you have no other resource but time and chance and change. Heaven knows, whatever sacrifices I could make how gladly should I make if they could promote your desires about her : it tears my heart to think that all sacrifices are *now* vain. Mary participates in my feelings—but I cannot write—

my   spirits   completely   overcome
me.—

> Your ever faithful
> and affectionate S.

Come and stay among us—If you
like, come and look for houses with
me, in our boat—it might distract your
mind.

LETTER XXIII.

[*Postmark :* PISA.
April 11*th*, 1822.]

Mary has not shown me her letter to you, and I therefore snatch an instant to write these few lines.

Come my best girl if you think fit, and assure yourself that every one—I need not speak for myself—will be most happy to see you :—But I think you had better wait a post or two, and not make *two* journies of it, as that would be an expense to no purpose, and we have not an overplus of money. In fact, you had better resolve to be of our party in the country, where we shall go the moment the weather permits; and arrange all your plans for that purpose.—The Williams's and we shall be quite alone, Lord Byron and his party having chosen Leghorn, where their house is already taken.

Do not lose yourself in distant and uncertain plans; but systematize and simplify your motions, at least for the present.

I am not well. My side torments me. My mind agitates the prison which it inhabits, and things go ill with me—that is within—for all external circumstances are auspicious.

Resolve to stay with us this summer, and remain where you are till we are ready to set off:—no one need know of where you are—The W's are serene people and we alone————

Before you come, look at Molini's what German books they have. I have got a Faust of my own, and just now my Drama on the Greeks'* is come—

* *Hellas.*

I will keep it for you.

Affectionately and ever yours,

S.

[*Addressed outside.*]
   Miss Clairmont,
      Presso al Prof.ᶜ Bojti,
         Piazza Pitti,
            Firenze.

LETTER XXIV.

Lerici, *Thursday.*
[*Postmark, Sarzana,* 31 *May,* (1822).]

My dear Clare,

I am vexed to hear that you are so ill, although the state of your spirits does not surprize me. I do not think there is any chance of your experiencing annoyance of whatever kind at Lerici, as I suspect between me and the only object from which it could spring there is a great gulph fixed, which by the nature of things must daily become wider.—I hear nothing of Hunt, nor have we any letters from England except those you are acquainted with and one from Mr. Gisborne.—I think you would be happier here; and indeed always either with or near me,—but on this subject your own feelings and judgement must guide you.   My health is much better this summer than it has been for many years; but the occupation of a few mornings in composition has somewhat shaken my nerves.—I have turned Maria's room into a study, and am in this respect very comfortable.—What do you think about the situation of the G's, and their pretensions upon our resources?   This question you cannot answer in a letter, but I should be very glad to hear your opinion on it: meanwhile I do nothing.—Mary has been very unwell.—She is now better and I suppose it will soon be necessary to make the Godwins a subject of conversation with her — at present I put off the evil day.—

The superscription of my poor boat's infamy is erased.   We have

had the piece taken out, and new reef
bands put in, and in such a manner
that it will be impossible to distinguish
that it has been mended; it merely
appears as if two additional reefs had
been inserted; of which indeed we
were greatly in want.—Jane, the other
day was very much discontented with
her situation here, on account of
some of our servants having taken
some things of hers, but now, as is the
custom calm has succeeded to storm,
to yield to the latter in the accustomed
vicissitude.—Mary though ill is good.
—And how are you?

I wish you could mark down some
good cook for us—a man of course.—
If you could find another Betta without the disagr[e]eable qualities of the
last it would do as well.

Your ever affectionate,

S.

Say when we are to come and meet
you.

[*Addressed outside.*]
       Miss Clairmont,
              presso al Sig^{e.} P^{e.} Bojti,
                    Piazza Pitti,
                           Firenze.

www.ingramcontent.com/pod-product-compliance
Lightning Source LLC
Chambersburg PA
CBHW020804020726
47495CB00008B/2584